I0734460

BUSINESS AS USUAL

CORPORATE COMMUNICATIONS IN THE ZOMBIE APOCALYPSE

JESSIE KWAK

Illustrated by
NATALIE METZGER

"Notes to Creative on the Fall 1 Catalog: Zombie Apocalypse Special Edition" first published in *Pedal Zombies: Thirteen Feminist Bicycle Science Fiction Stories,* September 2015.

"These 6 Jaw-Dropping Stats About Zombies Will Transform Your B2B Content Marketing Program" first published in *McSweeney's Internet Tendency,* April 2017.

"Don't Miss Today's Webinar on ExitZ, the World's Only Zombie Employee Offboarding Software Solution" also published in *Mad Scientist Journal: Autumn 2017.*

ISBN: 978-1946592026

CONTENTS

INTRODUCTION

Dear Reader,

I'm writing to you from a secure bunker near Pendleton, Oregon.

There's a certain desolate sort of beauty in eastern Oregon that inspires a longing in the soul. The vast plains, the wind rippling the grass, the entire weeks without seeing another human being....

It's the type of longing that is evoked by cowboy poets and in the radio dramatization of *Riders of the Purple Sage,* which I spent so many hours listening to in the back seat of my grandparents' Buick Park Avenue on road trips between Yakima and Walla Walla, Washington, when I was a kid.

It's a poetic longing, sure.

But mostly it's a longing for LTE cell service and the reliable internet connection I enjoyed in Portland.

Also I would kill for some Netflix.

Probably.

Best not to test me.

Like many of you, I've been concerned about the state of

content marketing ever since the first signs of the contagion showed up in Missoula. We had a rough start, but in the intervening year I've begun to feel hopeful. We may have lost several states entirely—not to mention a demoralizing number of microbreweries—but business is still going on as usual.

In my quest to document our new reality, I've spent the past year collecting stellar examples of how everyday businesspeople like you and me are keeping their chins up during the apocalypse:

In a transcript titled "Don't Miss Today's Webinar on ExitZ, the World's Only Zombie Employee Offboarding Software Solution," Chief Training Officer Margot Sanchez provides a very real-life demonstration of her company's early-warning system for employee zombieism.

In an email chain titled "Notes to Creative on the Fall 1 Catalog: Zombie Apocalypse Special Edition," Creative Director Joanna Ecco fights to meet the print deadline for her company's Fall 1 catalog, even while the world disintegrates around her.

And in a memo titled "Despite the Tragic Events of Day 2, I Think We Can All Agree Days 1 & 3 of GeoMundo's National Sales Meeting Were Transformational," National

Sales Manager Gerry Eltayeb gives us a glimpse into the insights—and chaos—of his company's annual national sales meeting.

I've also managed to collect other fragments of business as usual: conference brochures, leadership-training advertisements, and an all-staff company birthday email that proves festivity can still coexist alongside weapons trainings during hard times.

Taken all together, this collection is a testament to future generations that business does indeed go on.

May it inspire you to persevere yourself.

Take care out there,
And please send books and IPAs,

Jessie Kwak
Author, Ghostwriter, B2B Content Marketer, Human

BRAINCOOLER CHAT

ART BY NATALIE METZGER

Join us for UzXCon: the world's first user experience conference exclusively for zombie UX design!

Come network with your peers, learn from industry experts, and make sure your brand is on the leading edge of the zombie design revolution.

WE HAVE SOME AMAZING KEYNOTE SPEAKERS lined up!

KATIE CORD AND TIMOTHY W. LONG
Noted zombie horror writers and authors of
Leading with Brains: Surviving Middle Management in the Zombie Apocalypse

BRIAN STRADA
Chief Inspiration Officer at Synapstix Studios and author of

The Zombie Design Manifesto

BINNY ROY
Founder of ZombieDefense Solutions,
presenting his newest hands-on workshop:
*Designing with Daggers: Field Self-Defense Tactics for User
Experience Researchers*

It's not a conference—it's an experience!

Sponsored by:

- **ExitZ** — *The World's Only Zombie Employee Offboarding Software Solution*
- **BrainBubble**—*In-Store Analytics For An Apocalyptic World*
- **z.m.b**—*Innovation and Inspiration for the Undead*
- **Data Shuffler**—*The Only Data Analytics Platform Designed with Zombie Customers In Mind*

DON'T MISS TODAY'S WEBINAR ON EXITZ, THE WORLD'S ONLY ZOMBIE EMPLOYEE OFFBOARDING SOFTWARE SOLUTION

Good morning, everybody, and welcome to the webinar.

My name is Margot, and I'm the chief training officer for GreenLeaf HR Solutions. Today I'm just going to be going over some of the features of ExitZ, the world's only HR platform to combine a quick and painless zombie employee offboarding process with early-warning analytics to prevent further infections of your team.

Before we get started, I wanted to go over a couple of housekeeping items. First, I know you were all expecting to meet with our lead product innovator, Lauren. I'm sorry to say that, ah, Lauren isn't feeling great right now, so I've got her notes, and I'm stepping in.

You're in good hands.

Second, you should see a chat box to the right of the video. Can you all just let me know if you can see and hear me okay?

Mario, thanks. Thanks, Joanna. Great. Trish, Manoush, awesome. Thanks, everybody.

Paul, can you try closing your browser and relaunching the webinar? Everyone else seems to be seeing and hearing me fine. So just—

Okay, well, it looks like he closed out. Hopefully he can join us in a minute.

Okay.

Well.

While we're waiting for Paul, I just want to let you all know that you can leave any questions you have for me in the chat box. My assistant, Inez, is going to be flagging them all for me, and I'll answer them at the end. Okay?

I'm going to jump right in with some quick GreenLeaf history, which you may or may not know.

GreenLeaf has actually—you may know this—we've actually been developing Human Resources software solutions for over twenty years now. A lot of you are probably familiar with our flagship product, ZenHR.

Just a quick show of hands, can you click the "raise hand" button in the chat if you've used—or use—ZenHR?

Joanna, it's in the lower—sorry, let me check—yeah, the lower left part of the chat screen.

Oh, and hi, Paul, glad you can hear me now.

Technology, right, it's amazing except for when it's not working!

So, back to the history. About two years ago, when the first cases of zombieism were reported in Missoula, Green-Leaf was one of the first to realize just what a challenge it was going to be for HR directors to offboard zombie employees. Our product was actually in beta by the time the outbreak had gone national, and I'm proud to say we have over 3,500 users today.

Including, hopefully, you folks. So, thanks for checking out the webinar.

For those of you who've used ZenHR, you know that GreenLeaf is all about making your job easier. We know you have a lot going on.

Especially these days.

Now, I'm not going to ask for a show of hands here, but I know we've all probably had an experience or two with a zombie employee. If not, then you're definitely in the minority—and maybe knock on wood! The Association for Talent Development just released a study where they found six in ten HR managers have had to offboard at least one zombie employee in the past year. And one in five have had to offboard over five employees!

Obviously, those numbers are skewed regionally. Especially—do we have anyone here from Washington, Nevada, or Delaware?

No? Well, okay. We're just really sending good thoughts their way.

So, let's talk features.

Oops, let me just turn my phone off—so sorry about that. You get alerts for everything with some of these new smartphones; it drives me nuts. Technology, right?

Anyway.

With ExitZ, you're gonna find all the great offboarding features you need to make your job easier. Digital exit paperwork, of course, and—this is great—along with the usual exit forms, ExitZ also comes preloaded with all the latest forms from the Department of Zombie Labor. We hear all the time that this is a great feature, because the regulations can be confusing and you definitely want to make sure your business is compliant.

ExitZ also has an automated offboarding checklist to help zombie employees go through the process with minimal interaction with human staff. Plus, it's cloud-based, so your zombie employee can access the app securely off-premises from their own smartphone or tablet. Which, I guess I don't need to tell you how important all that is.

The next thing—and this is, I think, where our software really stands out—is the early-warning module. This integrates seamlessly with ZenHR, of course, but you can also use it on its own, or integrate it into whatever employee management system you're already using.

I will say—because I know I'll get this question at the end—it works on its own, but our early-warning module is much more effective when you've integrated it with some type of employee database. It doesn't have to be ZenHR—but it's just that the more data you have the easier it is to spot when somebody is starting to, well, turn.

It's actually designed to send both the HR team and the employee alerts, like—oh, haha, that's funny. Like this one that just showed up on my phone.

See what I said about alerts these days? They're constant.

Anyway.

The big thing you're gonna love about ExitZ is the exit survey.

Now, we all know that the exit survey is one of the most important pieces of information you can have when an employee leaves your company. But they're not always easy to get—especially not in cases of zombieism. That's why ExitZ actually sends multiple alerts to the ex-employee to remind them to take the survey.

We've designed the survey with really basic yes or no

questions and word associations that most Level I zombies can still comprehend. We worked with some of the best zombie psychologists and instructional designers to come up with this, and it's really actually very effective. How effective? About 68 percent better at getting responses than traditional exit surveys when it comes to Level I zombies, and 95 percent more effective for Level II zombies.

Which is pretty great, I think.

Once they're in the app itself—let me just pull up a screenshot here—you can see how the interface is really colorful and easy to navigate. The colors are designed to be attractive to zombie employees, which means no blue, of course. It's meant to draw them in.

They just want to, you know.

Open the app.

And tap the buttons.

Tap the buttons.

…Tap.

……Tap.

Where was I?

Right, so, next slide.

So sorry about that; it's been kind of a long week and it's only Tuesday! Haha.

Of course, as with every GreenLeaf product, we make ExitZ easy to customize. The software comes with a bunch of preloaded questions, but you can also write your own.

And, of course, all of this data goes straight into your dashboard, which is simple to use. Let me just pull it up….

You see how great these charts are, so easy to read. This is the kind of granular insight that can really help you grow your talent development program and avoid too much employee attrition to zombieism.

And, of course, it's really easy to export this data into all sorts of custom reports. You can even automate your weekly Centers for Disease Control reports, which I guarantee is gonna save you a lot of time. Those are a pain.

The last feature I want to talk about is...

Is...

I'm sorry, I'm just having a little trouble making out the words. I've been staring at a computer screen all day.

I think I have some eye drops here, just let me grab—

Inez? What are you doing?

I'm fine, I'm really.

It's allergies, it's—no!

Inez! NononoNO!

Hey, everybody! Um, this is Inez Martin, Margot's assistant. I, ah, just wanted to thank you all for sticking through to the end of the webinar and hope you appreciated that, ah, demonstration of just how effective the early-warning module can be.

Cool, so, I'm just going to skim through to the end of Margot's notes, and—yep, we're good. We've just about covered it.

I've been flagging your questions, so I guess I'll just dive in? Feel free to ask anything else you can think of in the comment section, and I'll tackle your questions as I see them.

I mean anything else about the *product*, though, actually.

Right—so, Paul, if the video is frozen, can you try logging out and logging back in? The rest of you can see and hear me, right? Yeah, okay, Paul, I think it might just be your computer again; I'm sorry about that.

But first, since a bunch of you have asked, yes, we'll be sending you a link to the recording of the webinar after— I'm sorry. I'm being told that we're not allowed— Excuse me, that we won't actually be sending this one out. Sounds like there was, ah, some sort of technical glitch in the recording?

That's too bad.

Um, but I will—just let me write this down—I'll be sure to send you a link to our resource library, which has a bunch of good links and stuff in it. And other webinar recordings, with our ex-lead product—I mean with our lead product innovator, Lauren.

Who's just out sick.

Does anyone have any questions?

NOTES TO CREATIVE ON THE FALL 1 CATALOG: ZOMBIE APOCALYPSE SPECIAL EDITION

From: Joanna Ecco <joanna@bikelifemarket.com>
To: Creative Team <CreativeStaff>
Re: Notes on Fall 1 Catalog

So far so good, people. Thanks for staying focused, I know it's been difficult with what's going on in the news. Also, has Tania checked in with anyone? Merchandising wants to add new product. This is not a good time for our photographer to be AWOL.

- **Raul** – I need to see finalized images by Wednesday. Consensus from Sales is to lose the blood spatters. Can you clone those out? Please tell me we don't need to reshoot.
- **Martina** – Enough with the Night of the Living Dead references in the product copy. Puns don't sell bikes. Specs sell bikes.
- **Steph** – Come by my office, let's go over cover options. Do we have any shots of the model where

she's showing more muscle? And Sales isn't into the shotgun poses, they say it confuses customers. We're a bike catalog, not a small arms dealer.

ADDED SKUs:

SKUs #41217 & #41218: We FINALLY got the sample product for the new Gore ZombieProof® Active Shell Jacket and Pants. **Martina**, product specs are on the Creative drive. Play up the bite-deterrent-yet-stylish stuff in copy, but Legal says don't make too many promises. **Steph**, shooting laydowns of these is priority one for Tania when she gets in. They're going on the commuter spread (44/45).

SKU #43189: XLC LazerBlade® Mini U-Lock. **Steph**, hi-res image is on the Creative drive. **Martina**, emphasize the safety features on this, we don't want people thinking the lasers will turn on in their back pocket anymore. XLC swears they've worked out that bug.

DROPPING SKUs:

The Bay Area has gone dark, so Merchandising doesn't think we can get any more Clif Bar product. Drop all carryforward Clif SKUs on the nutrition spread (32/33). Merch will turn over replacement items later this afternoon. Remaining Clif Bars will be stockpiled in the warehouse, but the news keeps saying it won't come to that around here, so no worries.

This is the approved copy for Model ZA-11 Ranger and the Model ZAP-13 UltraVolt:

RANGER: This tough-riding, indestructible commuter will get you through the Apocalypse. Hands down the most hassle-free bike on the market, with an ultra-silent Gates Carbon Belt Drive and low-maintenance Shimano Alfine Internal 11-speed rear hub. Comes standard with our patented indestructible titanium-zombonium® alloy disc brakes. Face the Apocalypse head-on when you add the optional collapsible gun rack and double Uzi holster. Steel. Colors: Lava, Espresso.

ULTRAVOLT: Endurance-race geometry combines with the latest in long-range electroshock weaponry for a high-voltage, high-adrenaline off-road bike. 27.5" wheels handle any obstacle they come across—as does the quick-fire VeNom® system. The 275-volt piezo-electric projectiles stun instantly, and with a range of 30 meters and up to 25 charges, *you'll* be the menace of your local trail system. Aluminum. Colors: Citrus, Aqua.

- **Martina** – Do we need to mention that Uzis aren't included with the Ranger? Sales is concerned. Lowest common denominator and all that. And I know you hate "zombonium." I know it's probably just the same alloy we've always used. But R&D says it's a thing, so we use it in copy. End of story.
- **Raul** – The graphics on the ZAP-13 need to really sizzle. Can you bring out the greens and yellows? Also, any way to show the stun gun thing in action?

Questions? I'll be in my office.

Thanks,
Joanna

From: Joanna Ecco <joanna@bikelifemarket.com>
To: Creative Team <CreativeStaff>
Re: Re: Notes on Fall 1 Catalog

- **Steph** – I talked to Kelvin in the warehouse about helping out in the photography studio since Tania hasn't checked in. Kid has an art degree, so he can probably figure out how to work a camera. Also, can you forward a press kit to that reporter from the B.R.A.I.N.?
- **Raul** – The retouched ZAP-13 graphics are perfect, thanks. Unfortunately, Production just told me they're changing them. See attached file. Can we clone those in? No time to reshoot.
- **Martina** – "Great minds taste alike"? When I said no Night of the Living Dead references, I also meant no references to Walking Dead or World War Z or any zombie puns AT ALL. It should go without saying that the headline for the components spread (48/49) will not be "Chaaaaaiiiinns." Keep it classy. We're in an apocalypse, people are dying. Don't make me give you a list of outlawed words.

ADDED SKUs:

SKU #48990: PDW BlueDiamond Taillight. **Steph**, Merchandising should have a hi-res image to you by this afternoon. **Martina**, Apparently it's a thing that they can't see the color blue. Roll with it. PDW has a FAQ page on their website with all the specs. Again, Legal says not to make any promises. Goes on electronics spread (46/47).

DROPPING SKUs:

ALL BELLS. Sending a separate email with specific info, but fyi apparently they really go crazy when they hear bells. Bells are out, going forward. **Steph**, come by my office and we'll discuss other options for the accessories page.
SKU #43189: XLC LazerBlade® Mini U-Lock.

- **Steph and Raul** – I sent you a meeting request, we need to talk about prAna's camouflage line. Do we have any other images from that shoot? I want the model to look more serene, but still wary. And the katana is overkill. Clone it out.

If you haven't heard the news, there now a contagion alert for the whole metro area. They're recommending that we all stay put, so the guys in the warehouse are sorting out sleeping and food arrangements. Talk to Operations if you have any questions, and pass the message on to your families.

Thanks,
Joanna

From: Joanna Ecco <joanna@bikelifemarket.com>
To: Creative Team <CreativeStaff>
Re: Re: Re: Notes on Fall 1 Catalog

This catalog is going to the printers on Saturday. This is a hard deadline, people. I expect to see all-nighters. And it's not like any of us have homes to get back to anyway.

- **Everyone** – If you see Tania DO NOT LET HER INTO THE BUILDING. Come see me if you have any questions.

ADDED SKUs:

SKU #49181: Burley BearCub Armored Baby Trailer. Going on the kids spread (16/17). Merchandising is working on getting hi-res images, but it sounds like things are getting tough in Eugene right now. **Steph**, can you find room in the spread? We can drop the Trail SnakPaks if we need space. **Martina**, we don't have any product sheets. I'm sure you can find everything you need for copy on Burley's website. **Steph and Martina** – Merchandising will be doing drive-by turnovers today to fill holes in the accessories spread (24/25). A handlebar-mounted motion sensor that CatEye just released, and couple handguns to cross sell with the Detours saddlebag holster. Turns out we're a small arms dealer after all. **Steph**, can we get these to Kelvin to shoot ASAP? **Martina**, Google the specs.

SKU #43189: XLC LazerBlade® Mini U-Lock.

(Online only) SKU #49908: Stainless Steel Katana. Will turn over this afternoon. This is the same katana from the prAna shoot. Sales thinks it's a good cross sell. **Raul**, can you add that back into the photos? Also, we just got the camouflage shipment, and the production colors are all completely different than the samples they sent us. You'll need to color correct. Merchandising will bring them by. **Martina**, this is online copy only, please add "katana available online" to the copy block for SKU #43353 (prAna Inner Strength Bullet-proof Camisole).

DROPPING SKUs:

SKUs #41217 & #41218: Gore ZombieProof items DO NOT WORK. Turns out they've been losing testers over there. Please replace with SKU #38990 Showers Pass Zombies Pass FlakJacket – pick up the copy and images from Summer 2.

Dinner's at 6 tonight, R&D is cooking spaghetti. Creative is excused from cooking shifts until all pages release to the printer. Attendance at weapons training demos is still required – next one is at 4:30 in the break room.

Back to work, people. We have a catalog to print.

Thanks,
Joanna

THE ARRIVAL OF THE APOCALYPSE DOESN'T HAVE to spell the end of your career!

Noted zombie horror writers Katie Cord and Timothy W. Long are back with a must-read take for any modern worker with ambition. With expert advice on professional development strategies for Level 1 and 2 zombies, managing interpersonal office dynamics between the living and undead, and how to be a boss who leads with brains—and heart.

Katie Cord is the author of *Maxine* and *He Left Her at the Altar, She Left Him to the Zombies*. www.katiecord.com

Timothy W. Long is the author of the Z-Risen series, the Broken Patriot series, and others. www.timothywlong.com

THESE 6 JAW-DROPPING STATS ABOUT ZOMBIES WILL TRANSFORM YOUR B2B CONTENT MARKETING PROGRAM

BY JESSIE KWAK

If the apocalyptic news pouring out of Missoula has you wondering about the fate of content marketing, you're not alone.

Thanks to a lot of brave (and mostly lucky!) researchers, a wealth of new studies has just been released about what zombies are consuming—content-wise, that is. And it's all great news for savvy B2B marketers who are looking to stay ahead of the horde.

If you've been unsure whether you should double down on your company's content marketing program during the zombie apocalypse, take a bite out of these 6 jaw-dropping statistics. Scientists may still be struggling to get a grip on the rapidly spreading outbreak, but one thing's for certain: The apocalypse is gearing up to be a game changer for B2B content marketing.

1. Among zombie B2B buyers, content consumption is up — way up.

Society may be crumbling around us, but a new study from DemandGen proves people are still hungry for content. Nearly half of B2B buyers reported reading 3-5 pieces of content before contacting sales; for buyers with zombieism, that number skyrockets to 27.

If you're wondering how you'll keep up with content demand, I have good news. According to a new EduCause survey, the average reading comprehension of a Level I zombie is only about third grade, and it drops by about 10 percent every month for Level II zombies. Just focus on creating snackable pieces with plenty of graphics to ensure your message is easily communicable.

2. Zombies have no short-term memory, so go ahead and repurpose existing content

Marketers rejoice—there's a silver lining in the end-times! A recent survey by HubSpot found that Level I zombies were only able to accurately recall content they'd read in the last *five minutes*. So go ahead and bring your best pieces of content back from the dead. A zombie buyer won't know the difference.

Plus, Curata reports that only 29 percent of marketers are currently repurposing content—which means this is great low-hanging fruit if you want to beat back your competitors.

3. Auto-play videos remain the number 1 cause of death in public libraries

Despite repeated warnings from the CDC and Content Marketing Profs, an astonishing 28 percent of companies are still using auto-play videos on their B2B sites.

Which we all know by now can trigger berserker rage in zombie users, folks. It's time to decapitate this trend for the sake of all our sanity—and in the interest of public safety.

4. Social media is not just for millennials

According to Social Media Examiner, 42 percent of Level I zombies have active Twitter accounts and tweet at least 5 times each day. Surprisingly, that number goes up to 23 times per day for Level II zombies. About two thirds of those are retweets, which means the possibility of your content going viral is huge.

B2B marketers need to be paying attention here, especially since Forrester reports that 68 percent of buyers—both zombie and human—have made purchases based on recommendation on social media.

5. Zombies are fanatical about brand loyalty

That same Forrester report shows that 85 percent of zombies reported they were more likely to buy a product they had used before they contracted zombieism than one they hadn't tried.

Surprisingly, that percentage goes up 7 points as zombies progress from Level I to Level II. This suggests that zombies tend to seek out the comfort of past experiences the further they get from humanity—and might just turn into your biggest brand advocates.

Savvy B2B brands should focus on the delight factor in order to create infectious loyalty in zombie customers as they devolve.

6. The zombie buyer journey has some unusual twists and turns

You're already mapping your content to the buyer journey— but don't forget to map it to the zombie devolution journey, as well. Whereas the majority of human B2B buyers surveyed by Marketbridge preferred to reach out to sales via phone or email, *97 percent* of zombie buyers preferred to stalk the salesperson to their home.

This presents some fascinating new opportunities to keep your brand "top of brain." Think yard signs, posters, and even guerrilla tactics like sidewalk chalk.

The fate of the world may be bleak, but the future of content marketing is brilliant!

As their competitors struggle to cope with the apocalypse, forward-thinking B2B marketers are looking at the content marketing opportunity of a lifetime. This is your chance to turn your brand into an industry leader—so stay safe out there, and keep creating amazing content!

If nothing else, we'll all need plenty to read while we're in hiding from the hordes.

From: Margot Sanchez <msanchez@greenleafhr.com>
To: Jessie Kwak <jessie@jlkwak.com>
[OUT OF OFFICE] Re: Interview request: Article on zombie employee offboarding challenges

Hello!

Thank you for your inquiry!

I'm currently away from the office for personal leave, but I will respond to your email as soon as I am able.

If you have any questions about implementing ExitZ, the world's only zombie employee offboarding software solution, please contact my assistant, Inez Martin at imartin@greenleafhr.com.

If you have any questions regarding the wholly uneventful webinar of April 16th, please get in touch with Todd Boren at pr@greenleafhr.com.

Sincerely,
Margot Sanchez

CTO
GreenLeaf HR Solutions
HR Made Personal—for humans and non-humans alike.

From: Paula Than <paula.than@datashuffler.com>
To: AllStaff <AllStaff>
Re: April birthday celebrations & special flame thrower training Tuesday at 3pm

To the team,

Happy April! I've been excited to see the crocuses come up in the parking strip—it's so nice to see spring on its way. I know it's been a long winter since the contagion hit, but I want to thank you all for your dedication and perseverance. It hasn't been easy working together *and* living together!?!

Speaking of, let's give a big shout-out to Wayan and Amir for hosting all those poker nights!

Our birthday list for April is a bit shorter this year, so we'll be combining our usual monthly birthday party with the weekly weapons training.

Come down to the cafeteria to celebrate Jeff, Alexis and Joel with cupcakes and a special surprise—a case of LaCroix that Missy in Accounting scavenged from Safeway! Thank you, Missy!

Afterward, Teresa from Operations will demonstrate proper flame thrower technique and go over basic safety procedures. It ought to be fun—you won't want to miss! Also, weapons trainings are mandatory.

Remember, as always, optional advanced training sessions

are always available with Teresa. And don't forget to sign up for next week's session, which she'll be co-teaching with special guest Binny Roy. It's called *Big Data Ballistics: Practical Munitions for Programmers and Systems Admins.* Space is limited!

Thanks!!
Paula Than

Human Resources Director
Data Shuffler
The Only Data Analytics Platform Designed with Zombie Customers in Mind

KILLING TIME

ART BY NATALIE METZGER

MEMO:

Good morning!

I'd like to thank you all for attending this year's rather memorable National Sales Meeting last week. For those of you who have been asking, Diego was declared 100 percent clear from infection. He'll be released from the biocontamination ward this afternoon and should be back at work Monday morning. So we can all breathe a sigh of relief there.

First off, I want to thank Monique for taking over the organization of the meeting after Toby's unanticipated devolution into Level 2 zombieism. His were hard shoes to fill, especially after the shenanigans during the wonderful "buyer objection" scavenger hunt he organized for last year's meeting.

With that in mind, I think we can all agree Monique did a terrific job with such short notice.

I know there has certainly been some tension between the sales and marketing departments since the beginning of the apocalypse last August, but I think this was a great opportunity for us all to come together and see each other's perspectives. In particular I'd like to offer thanks to our CMO Gloria for the presentation on in-person techniques for overcoming the objections of prospective Level 1 zombie buyers, and to special guest Binny Roy for the follow-up demonstration of appropriate self-defense tactics.

Unfortunately, Carlos's great presentation on the rebranding of our MountainPro line of GPS units to compete in the emerging zombie avoidance market was cut short by hordes breaking through our meeting room defenses. But that just led to a fantastic real-life demonstration of self-defense by Binny Roy. It was great to see that his techniques really held up in a real-world scenario.

Here's a link to Carlos's complete PowerPoint deck, and for those of you who are free tomorrow at 3pm Eastern, Carlos will be answering questions on a conference call. I'll be sending a meeting request to you all with the call-in information.

And for those of you who are interested in learning more self-defense—and I think we all should be—Binny has generously offered us a discount for his in-person class: *Dueling with Buyers: Sales and Swordsmanship for Zombie-Facing B2B Sales Pros*. Talk to Manoush in HR if you'd like to sign up.

That said, on behalf of the entire management team, I'd like to reiterate that GeoMundo values the safety of our sales team above all else. Don't put your humanity in danger just to reach your quotas. If you feel pressured to do so, we encourage you to speak with HR anonymously.

On a lighter note, we'd also like to recognize our Salespeople of the Year Award winners, Annie Hua and Seth Lamond. In particular we want to recognize their innovative use of everyone's favorite party game, Cranium, to get their message across to Level 2 zombie buyers. That quick thinking helped Annie and Seth open one of our biggest accounts of the year—and come out of the meeting completely unscathed. I think we all have a lot to learn from those two.

And, finally, the containers with our summer product have all been rerouted once again to Tacoma after the CDC declared Los Angeles a Class 4 biocontainment area, so let your dealers know the new estimated shipping dates and thank them for their ongoing patience with the zombie apocalypse.

I hope you all got as much out of the National Sales Meeting as I did. I encourage you all to familiarize yourself with the new catalogue, which includes our most current offerings for both zombie avoidance and hobby aviation. And keep an eye out for the new marketing collateral, which should be on your doorstep soon.

By the way, if you're no longer able to accept delivery at your home—particularly those of you in Washington,

Nevada, or Delaware—please let Monique know and we'll arrange delivery wherever you've found refuge.

I'll talk to you all on Monday morning for our weekly check-in. Thanks, everyone, and stay safe out there.

Gerry Eltayeb

National Sales Manager
GeoMundo GPS
Your world, in your hand

BRAINSTORMING SESSION

ART BY NATALIE METZGER

ABOUT THE AUTHOR

Jessie Kwak is a human B2B marketing copywriter and novelist who sometimes amuses herself by imagining how much more lively corporate communications would be during the time of the zombie apocalypse. Her short fiction has appeared in *McSweeney's Internet Tendency* and *Bikes in Space vols. 1—4*, among other places; her non-zombified B2B marketing writing has appeared in *Venture Beat, CMI,* and on the websites of various SaaS clients; and you can find her paranormal and gangster sci-fi novels on her website, jessiekwak.com.

Her next project has her traveling to Missoula to conduct a survey on brand communication best practices at the heart of the contagion. It will be released in the spring, providing we even hear from her again.

We wish her luck.

CONNECT WITH JESSIE

Ghostwriting & Editorial Services: BasslineEditorial.com
B2B Content Marketing: jlkwak.com
Fiction: jessiekwak.com
jessie@jessiekwak.com
@jkwak

ABOUT THE ILLUSTRATOR

Natalie Metzger is a human illustrator with more than a decade of experience working in a variety of mediums. Natalie is the cartoonist behind several webcomics including Cthulhu Slippers and Over-Encumbered.

Her illustration work focuses on creepy cute comic-style drawings with a preference for pen, ink and tentacles.

Natalie is available for illustration, art events, commissions and projects.

Connect with Natalie

Website: www.thefuzzyslug.com
natalie@thefuzzyslug.com
@minitotoro

combatant by the Indiran Alliance. Willem Jaantzen is a notorious crime lord about to end a fearsome vendetta—and most probably his life. When he learns his goddaughter has been captured by the Alliance, will he be able to save her? And her, him?

GET IT FOR FREE AT JESSIEKWAK.COM!

Manu Juric is a mediocre bounty hunter. But he's damn good at reading people and creating unexpected explosions — and that can take you a long way in this business. Just not far enough, he learns when he tries to take out one of Bulari's most notorious crime lords: Willem Jaantzen.

Available in print, ebook, and audiobook.

www.ingramcontent.com/pod-product-compliance
Lightning Source LLC
Chambersburg PA
CBHW032052180726

48284CB00004B/1301